Dedicated to
Dax, Dylann, Hunter and Quin

... and Laura

Chapter I

The day started off, as days often do,
with a stretch and a yawn and a brush and a poo.

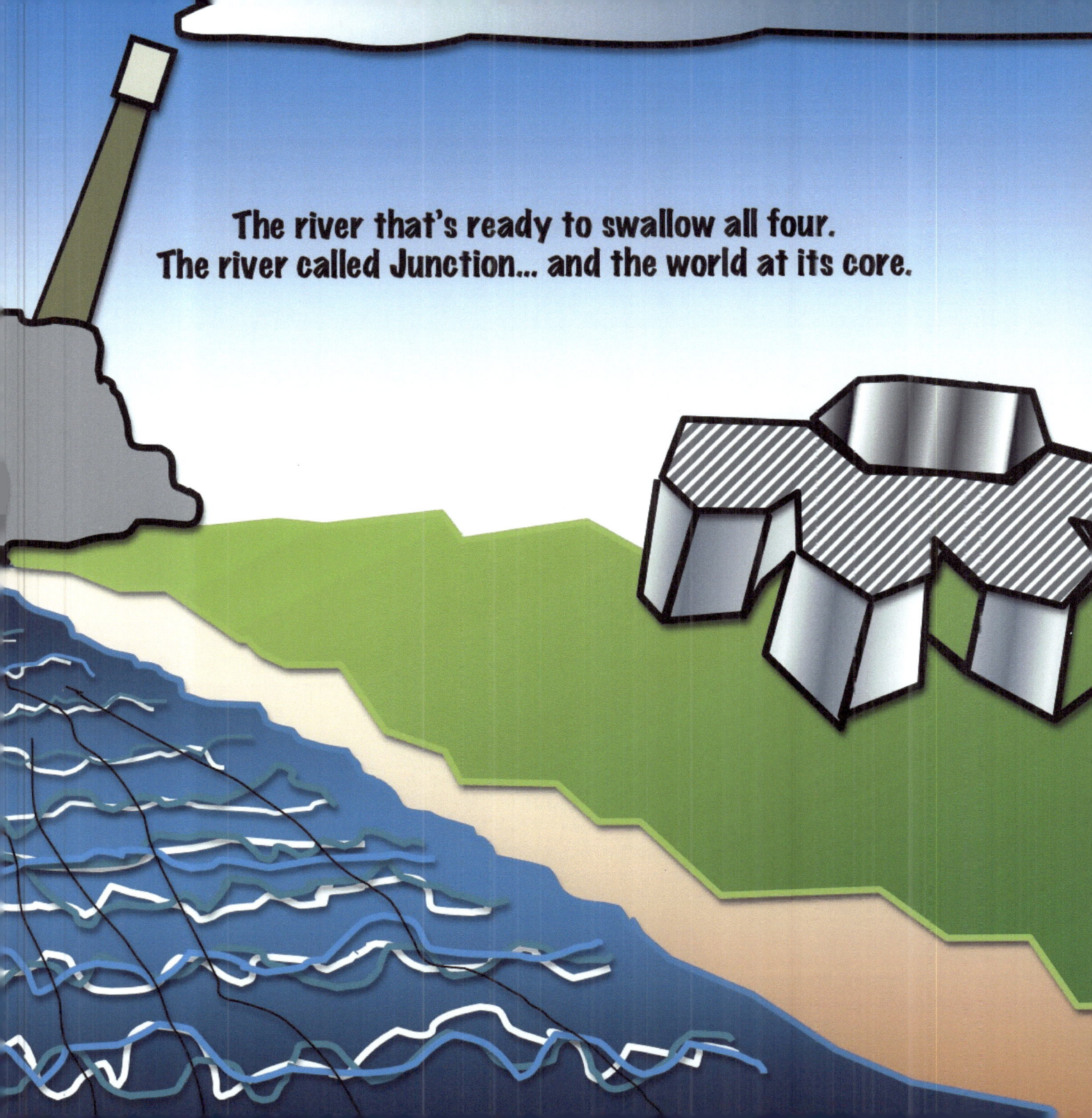

So went Hunter and Dylann, and her brothers too,
Dax busy dancing and Quin with one shoe,
somewhere between what's not and what's true,
to the river that rushes, as most rivers do.

If only they'd known what kind of river this was,
where Dylann sat thinking the things Dylann does,
where Dax kept on dancing cause that's what he loves,
and Quin was still laughing at Hunter because...

Quin was just doing what Quins often do.
They laugh at what's funny and walk with one shoe.
Though some of these things a boy can undo,
laughing's not something Quin ever outgrew.

Quin's bright side was something that couldn't be lost.
So, when his shoe floated by down the river that tossed,
"No Quin!" Dylann cried though he laughed when she bossed.
Quin wanted his shoe and he'd get it back at all cost!

Quin stood up laughing and wore such a grin,
that Dylann and Dax knew that Quin would jump in!
AND HE DID!
Dax followed so fast it would make your head spin.
For, if a game could be won, it was Dax who would win.

Though Dax was quite quiet with adults around,
all alone he was brilliant and brave he had found.
SO INTO THE WATER! and swept underground.
Dax was a hero and Dylann just frowned.

See, Dylann knew better. She was used to those two.
Two boys who knew better but still did what they do.
She rolled her eyes and jumped after. Well, what would you do?
Which is the question that Hunter was wondering too.

Hunter didn't do anything but not out of fear.
He was brave and courageous but his path was unclear.
His cousins, all screaming, was all he could hear.
When their voices went quiet, so did he disappear.

Chapter II

The river splished them and splashed them like toilet flushes.
For very few rivers move like this river rushes.

A river that rushes the way rivers do,
with one girl extra and her brothers too,
who saw Hunter vanish through the grate he watched through,
through the grate on the river like a cage in a zoo.

Hunter had vanished! How crazy it sounds,
through the grate that grew smaller and as they splish-splashed around,
down a river that dragged them deep deep underground,
as they flitted and floated and tried not to drown.

It took, like forever, to wash up on dry land,
Dylann's hair all ditz-frizzy, Quin's shoe in his hand,
on the shores of a world they did not understand,
this was not turning out like the day they had planned.

Dax was the first upon shore, you can bet,
near dank things and dark things they hadn't met yet.
What he heard, when he stood there, he'd never forget,
a voice, from the dark, said,

"Who's that!" Dylann shouted which gave Dax a fright.
So dank there, so dark there, much darker than night.
As dark as, above ground, Hunter thought that it might.
So he'd opened a manhole and dropped a flashlight.

It fell, like a star, through the dark in bright flashes.
Hunter knew, if you threw it, Dax always catches.

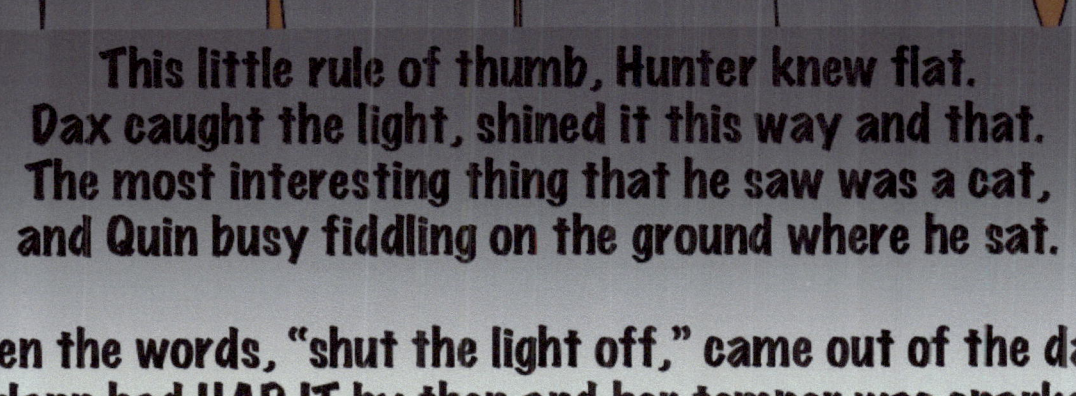

This little rule of thumb, Hunter knew flat.
Dax caught the light, shined it this way and that.
The most interesting thing that he saw was a cat,
and Quin busy fiddling on the ground where he sat.

When the words, "shut the light off," came out of the dark.
Dylann had HAD IT by then and her temper was sparked.
She shouted, "WHO'S THERE!" and stepped to her mark.
Dax backed her up, "Yeah! Who's there!!?" he barked.

Whosever that voice was, Quin already knew.
He laughed cause he knew it, as Quins seem to do.
His uncle had told him so he knew it was true.

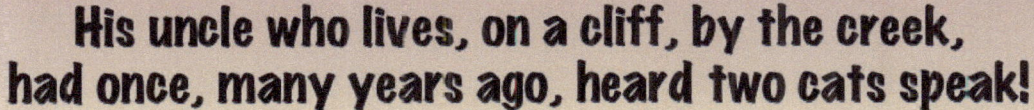

His uncle who lives, on a cliff, by the creek,
had once, many years ago, heard two cats speak!

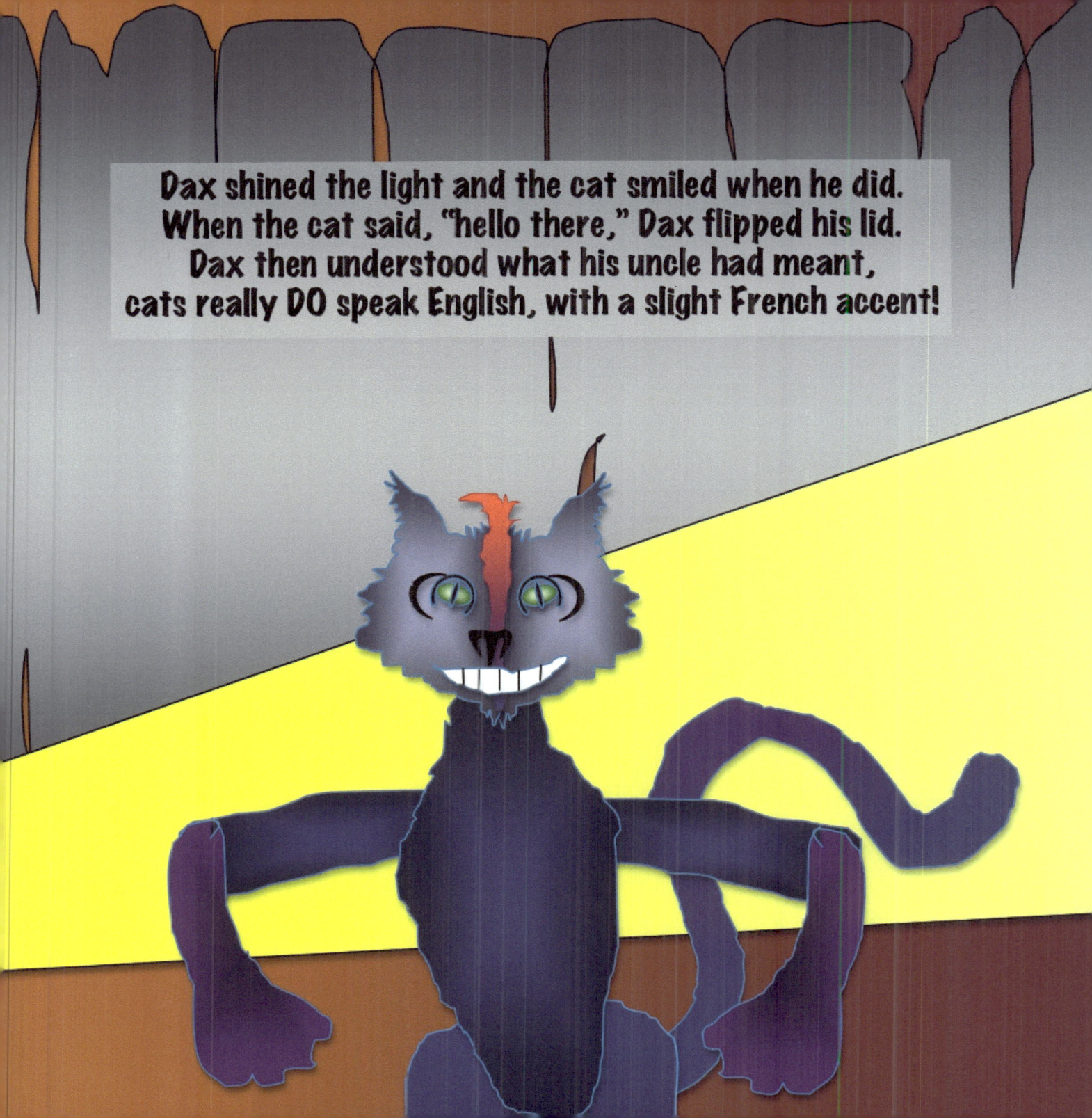

But Dylann knew better and asked with much grace,
"Excuse me sir, cat sir, please help us out of this place?"
The cat said, "my eyes hurt," with his paws on his face.
So Dax turned the flashlight and flashed it away
to where Quin stood, wearing both his shoes... AND A CAPE!

Now, most of the time cat's don't care at all.
But this cat loved mischief and walked to the wall.
"There's a hole there," he said to them all,

"There's a hole there,
but you can't go there,
you're too fat and too tall."

Chapter III

Quickly the cat jumped down the hole like a champ.
But none of these kids could be told what they can't.

Besides if you do it, then that's what you do.
They believed in themselves and the things that they knew.
You just have to do it, it's all up to you.
SO INTO THE TUNNEL! and all the way through.

Dax had the flashlight so he went in first.
Then Quin who was smallest and tooted the most.
Dylann just fit with her face in the dirt,
with her face right near Quin's cape, which could be the worst!

They weaseled their way as they weaseled along,
getting pinched in and flattened like they didn't belong.

They popped from the hole with strange looks on their faces,
into a strange world that was clearly the strangest,
where light from the flashlight bounced into bright lasers,
and comets and starfalls, and the kids were stargazers.

Until, Dax felt the swap of a soft little fist,
that knocked the flashlight right out of his wrist.
"The light hurts our eyes, please kindly desist.
We'll trade you some cat's eyes for socks you won't miss."

See, yarn is a thing that cats cannot resist.
For their yarnballs, they'll take it, whatever the risk.

With cat goggles on, and their feet newly bare,
the children could finally see where they were,
in a pocket of nickel, with cats everywhere,
cats wearing capes as all cats these days wear.

"That kid stole my cape!" squeaked a voice from the crowd,
but nobody heard. Dax said, "WOW!" way too loud,
which Quin seemed to find the most laughable sound,
so he "WOWed" too and laughed at the world they had found.

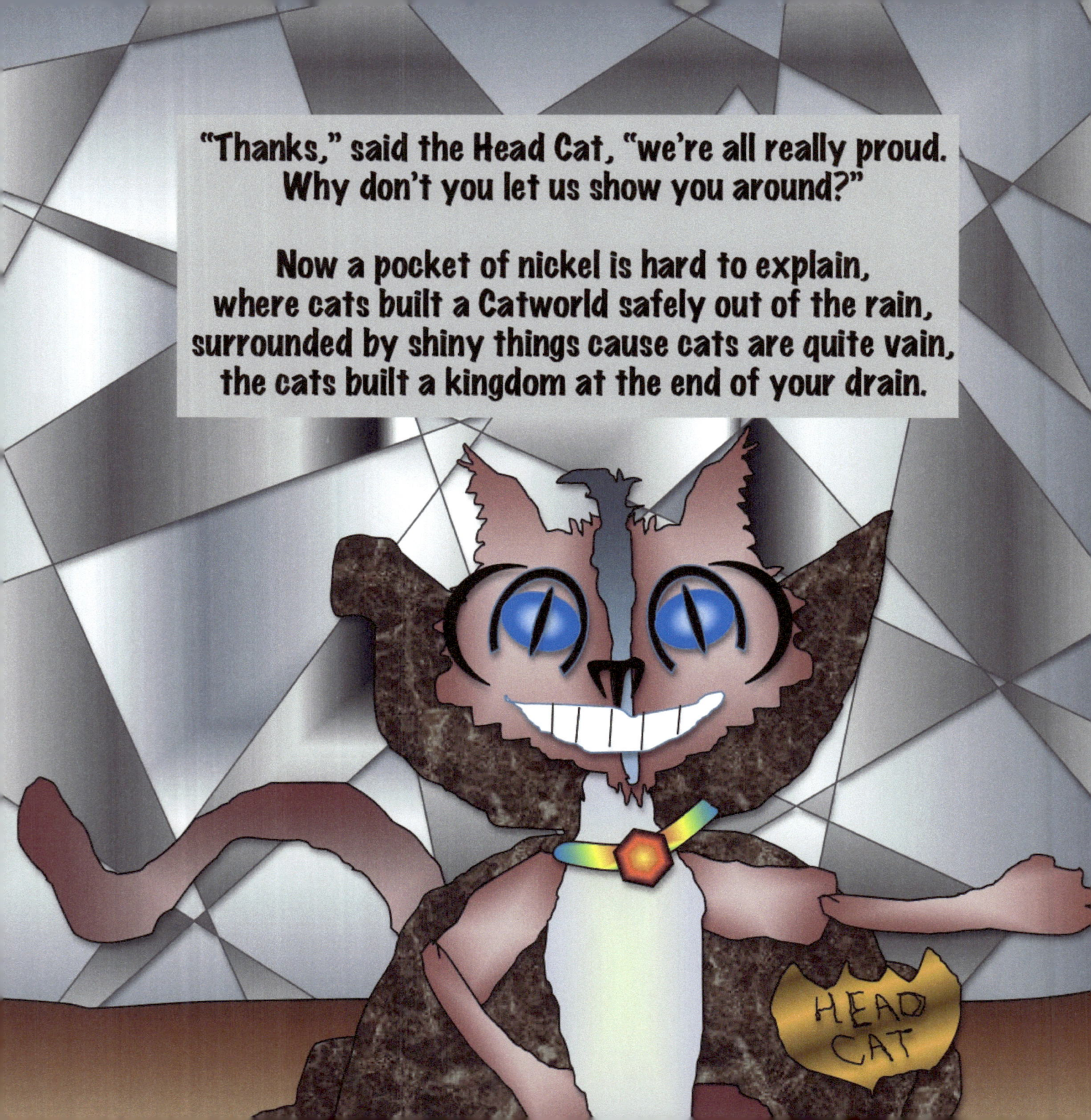

You wouldn't believe what the cats have done.
In a cavern of nickel, full of balls of yarn.

"Here's the powerhouse. We use our power quite fairly.
We understand your dilemma, so we use this quite rarely.
See, the core is a magnet and, when we plug it in,
it sucks just one sock out of every machine!

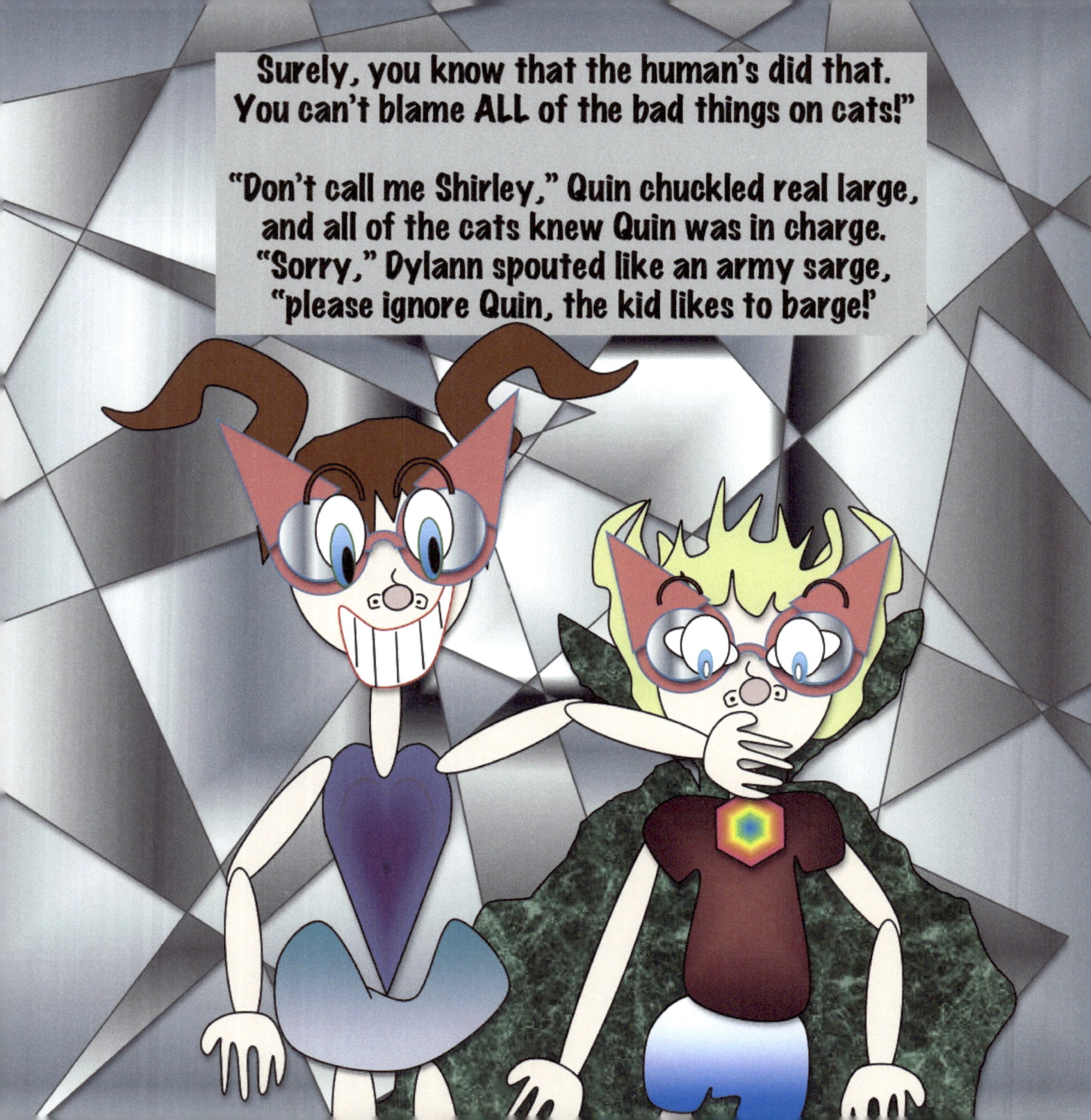

"Go on," Dylann said though she already knew
that time was real close to their late night curfew.
"We did build the smoke stack, yes that part is true,
cause smoking is one of the bad things cats do.

HEAD
CAT

The watertower is our satellite dish.
And Ramsey's where we keep our fish.
In shiny warm yarnholes we do what we wish.
Rub our fur, hear us purr, this is bliss."

Chapter IV

Quin whipped his cape up in the air like a sheath.
Don't worry, he still had more capes underneath.
The cats just meowed there in cat disbelief.
They'd forgotten that children cause cats so much grief.

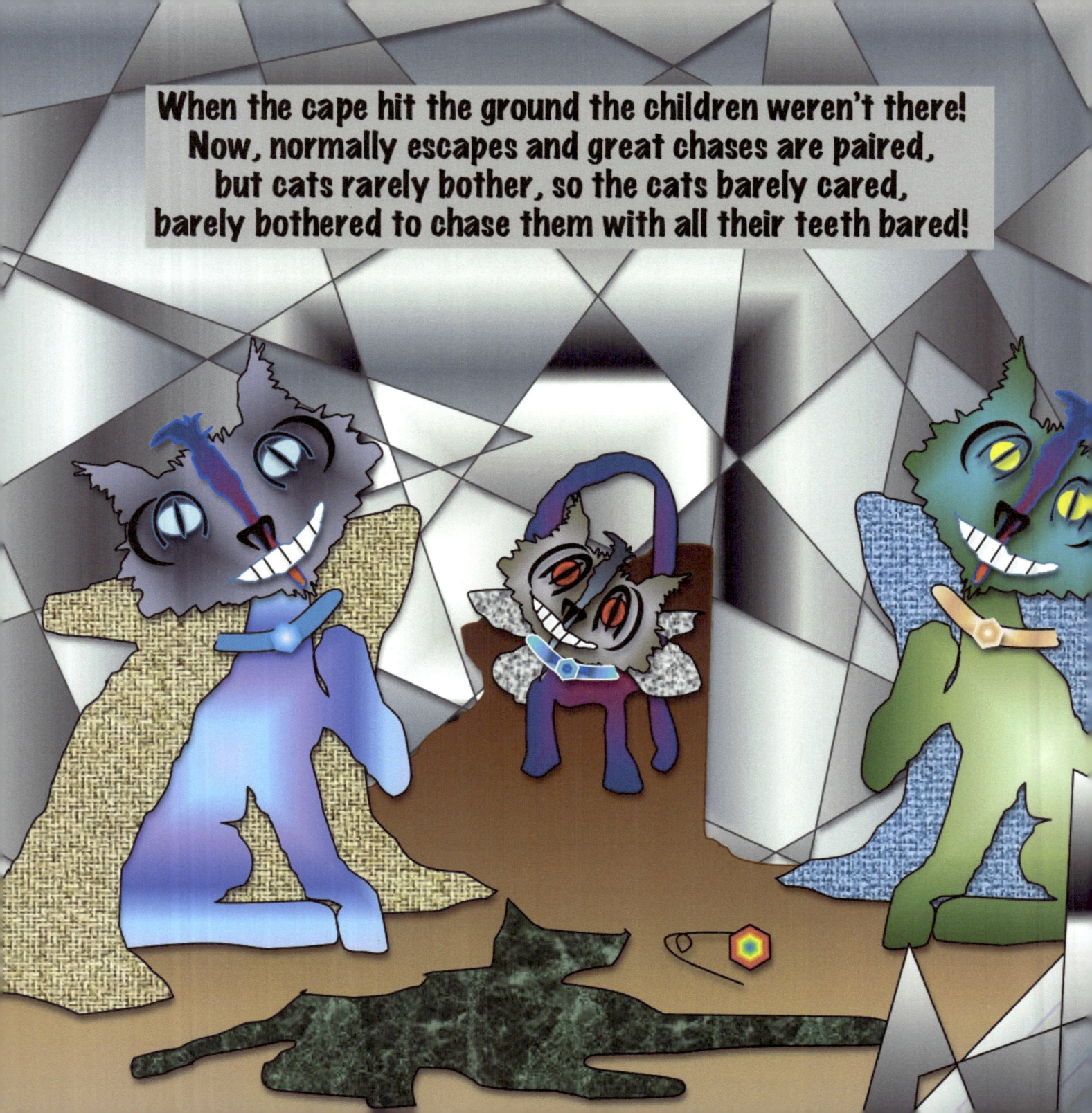

While the children, on yarnmounds, slid down nickel slides.
They slid down, and slipped round, and rode the wild ride.
They couldn't have had any more fun if they tried
and they laughed, when it ended, cause nobody'd died!

Though clearly the cat's idea kinda smelled,
Dylann got in first and kept her tongue held,
then Dax in, then Quin in, as air currents swelled.
They sounded like three little girls when they yelled

They yelled as they lifted and drifted on by,
as they lifted and shifted up into the sky,
till they'd risen, still whizzing, up up way too high,
Dax and Quin laughing, and Dylann pie-eyed!

Suddenly, above them, they heard their yells answered,
Dax hip-hopped it up cause he's a good dancer.
With a stick, Hunter reached like a champion lancer.
He poked Dylann's butt first, the next time he pantsed her.

Hunter had yelled down each manhole he'd spied.
While invisibly adventuring on the top side
of a Catworld built with cattools and catpride,
a nickel and yarn world, cats tried hardly to hide.

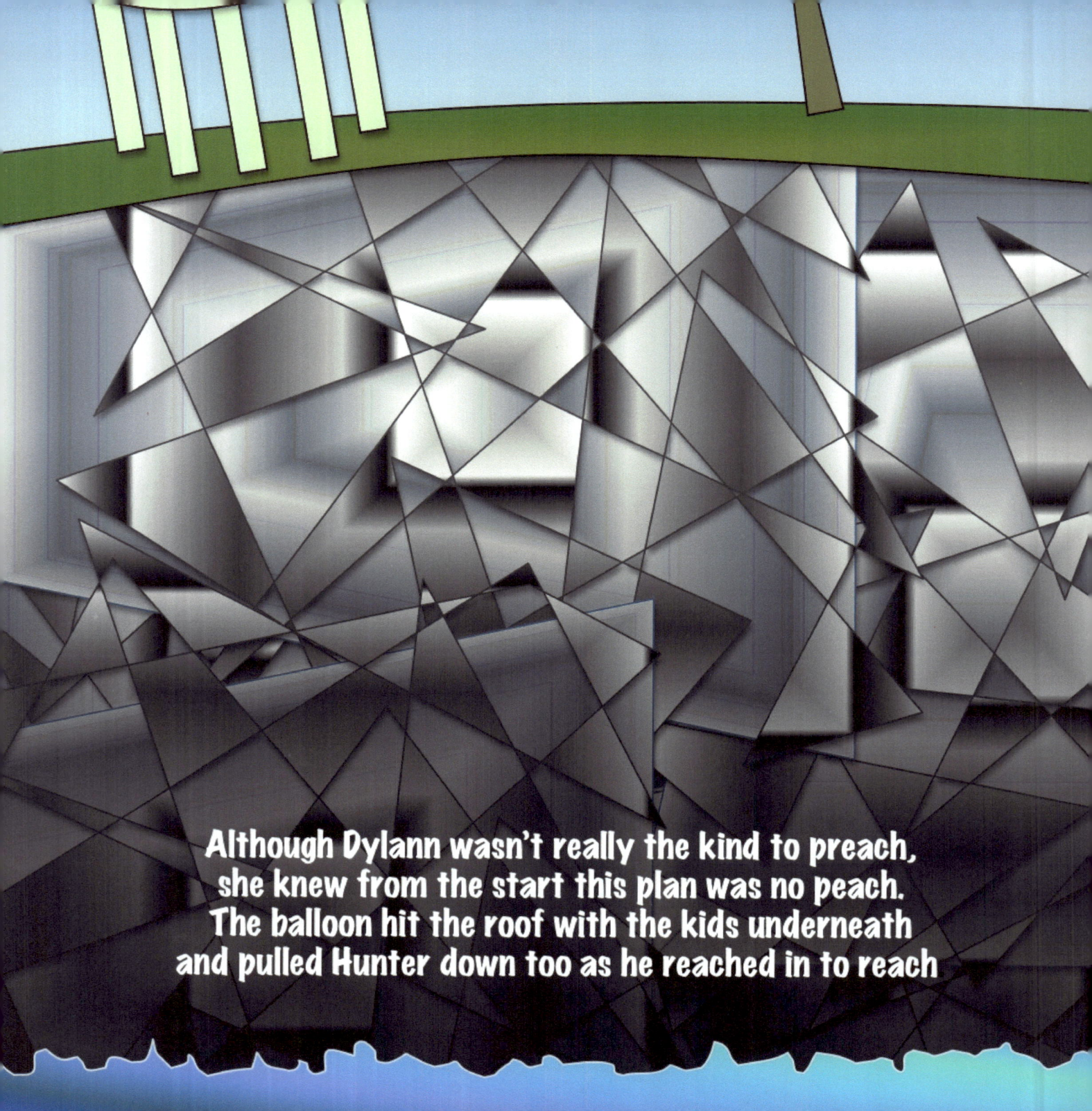

Although Dylann wasn't really the kind to preach,
she knew from the start this plan was no peach.
The balloon hit the roof with the kids underneath
and pulled Hunter down too as he reached in to reach

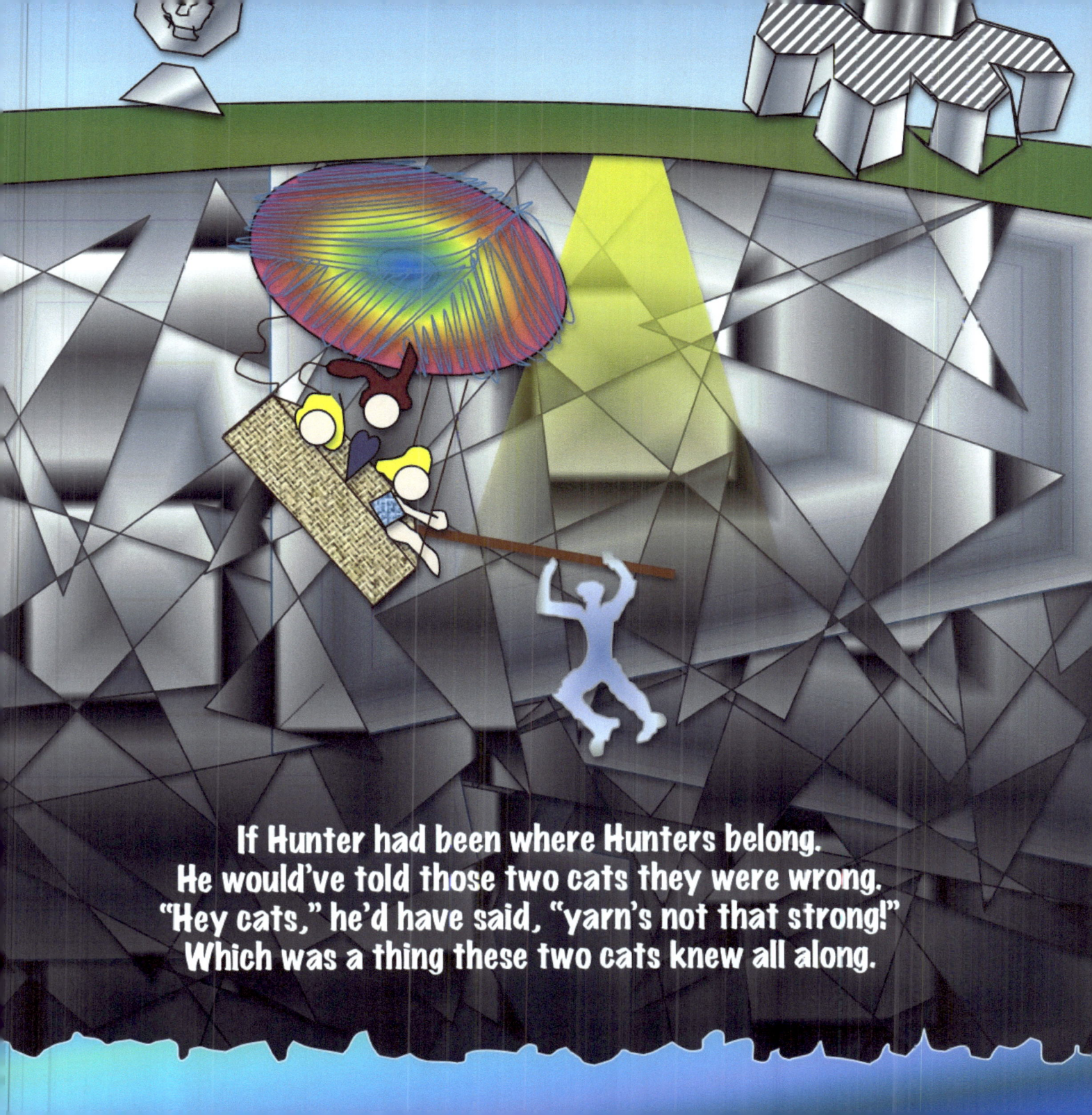

If Hunter had been where Hunters belong.
He would've told those two cats they were wrong.
"Hey cats," he'd have said, "yarn's not that strong!"
Which was a thing these two cats knew all along.

The cats knew the way out depended on Quin,
because the only way out is the way you got in,
and what you can do with a cape with a pin,
what Quins can do, and why all Quin's grin.

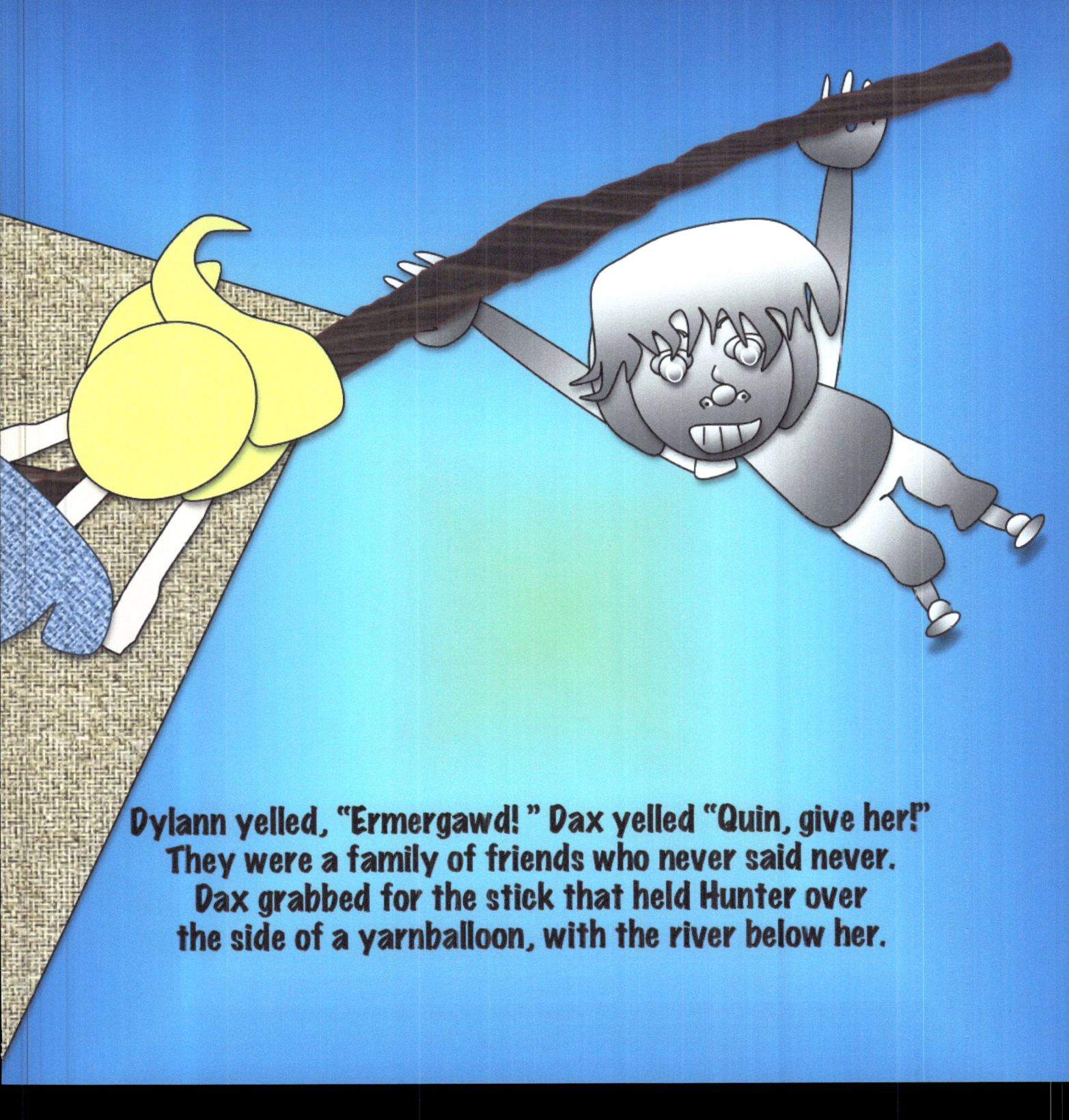

Dylann yelled, "Ermergawd!" Dax yelled "Quin, give her!"
They were a family of friends who never said never.
Dax grabbed for the stick that held Hunter over
the side of a yarnballoon, with the river below her.

They splashed down in front of all of the cats.
Into Junction creek and back on their path.
What once was balloon was suddenly raft,
on its way out of Catworld incredibly fast.

Quin stood back up with a fish on his head.
And all the cat's laughed in their yarns made of beds.
"I'm cool," was the cool thing Quin coolly said.
Then Dax laughed, then Hunter, and Dylann turned red.

Back on Junction Creek with a balloon for a raft,
getting upchucked and chucked down, tossed this way and that,
the kids had all HAD IT! with worlds made by cats.

Where, once, capes were in fashion.
Now, where cats wore fishhats.

Chapter V

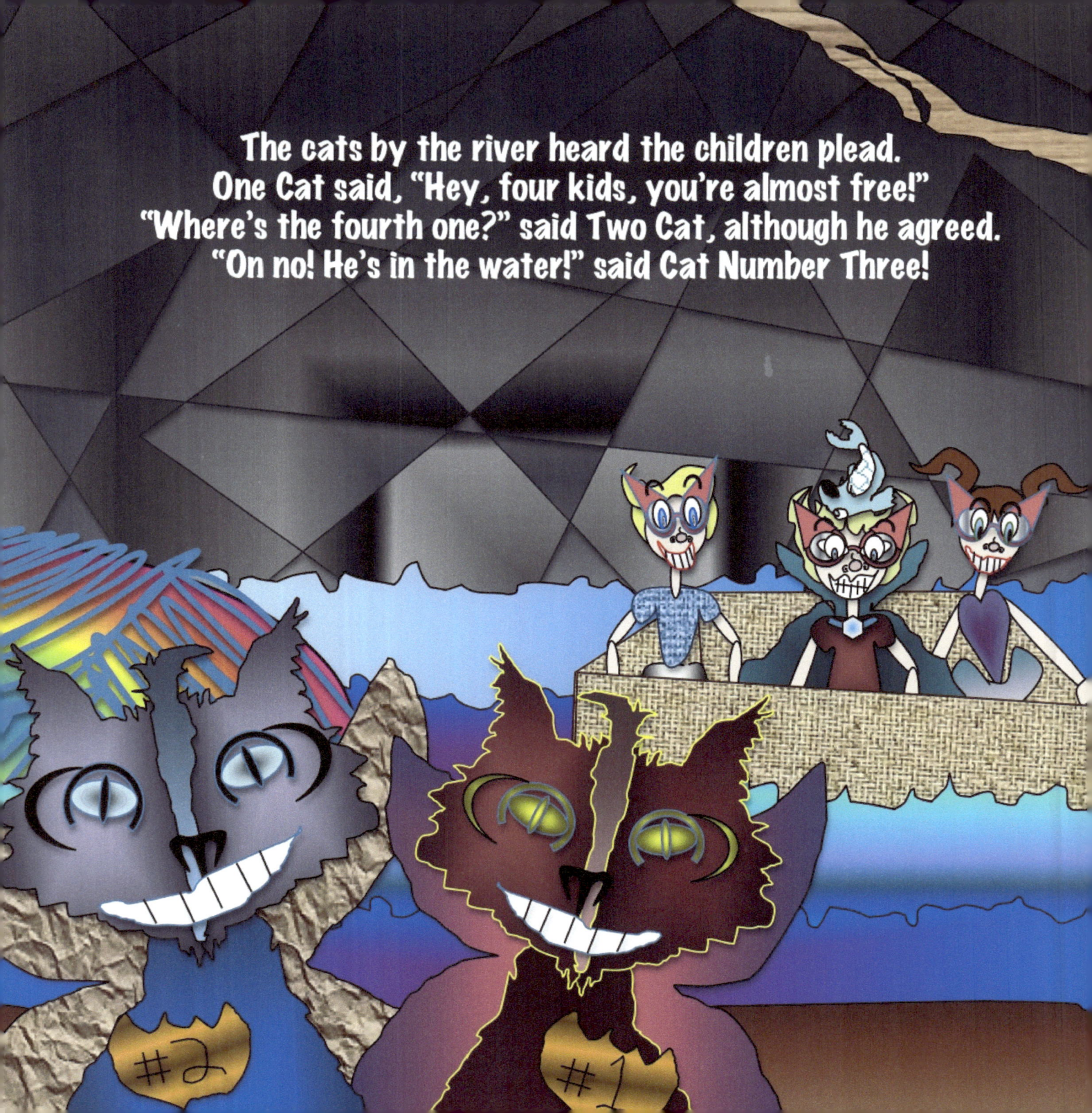

The cats by the river heard the children plead.
One Cat said, "Hey, four kids, you're almost free!"
"Where's the fourth one?" said Two Cat, although he agreed.
"On no! He's in the water!" said Cat Number Three!

"Hunter, where are you? Why can't I see you?"
"Right here in the basket, it really is me who...
I figured it out, I think I found the key to
making me clear again and who I might be too.

"Oh for Cat's sake!" shouted Cat Number Three,
"you can be whatever you want to be.
Just like you, I'm just me. Every cat is that free.
You just have to choose. To choose, is the key!"

Then Number Three puffed on his cat cigarette,
trying catlike to keep it from getting too wet.
So this is how Hunter and Number Three met.
And started adventures you haven't seen yet!

Which was a wonderful thing to have happened,
to cousins and brothers and sisters and fast friends.
This is the way their adventure-filled day ends,
since Number Three Cat knew each of the creek bends,

and siphons and rapids and water spouts,
cats are far too clever to ever doubt,
that cats don't already know all about,
steering yarnballoon rafts all the way out.

Junction Creek had pulled them down to the core,
gave them all they could handle and not a bit more,
showed them a crazy new wonderful Catworld before
it blitzed them and spit them back onto the shore.

Quin chased after what his little heart yearned,
and although everybody else kinda got burned,
back on the shore, once they'd been safely returned,
they laughed and they joked about what they'd all learned.

Dax pumped a fist and said, "Man! That was sweet!"
Quin took his cape off, "I'm hungry, let's eat."
Then Dylann said, "yeah, let's get back on our feet."
Number Three started, "sure was a pleasure to meet..."

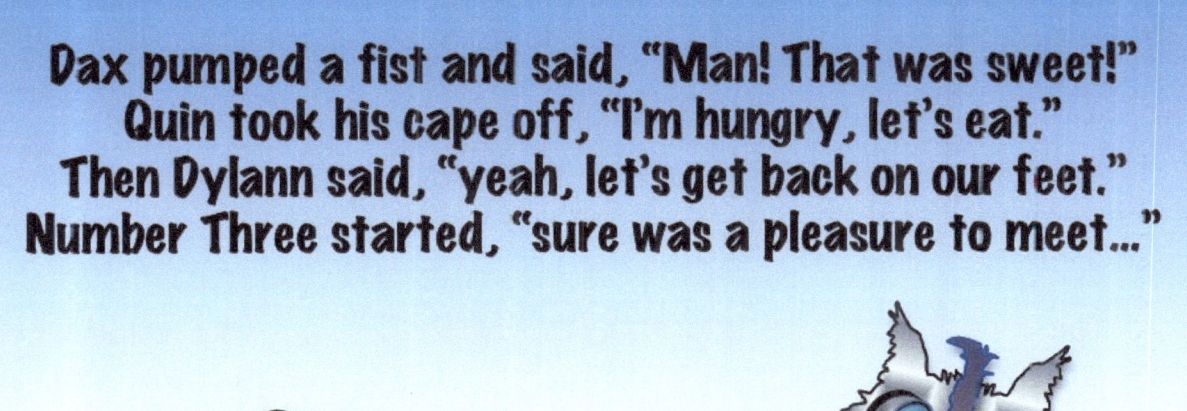

Now, if a story needs a moral, then we're on the brink.
But no one should tell you what you should think.
So decide who you are and get ready to wink,
cause the whole world can change in the speed of that blink.

Time spent is time that belongs to the spender.
If you see a friend hurt then jump in to defend her.
Dare everyday! Spend your days in adventure!
Your craziest dreams can be days you remember.